I0581983

RED CHRONICLES
SERIES PREQUEL

REQUITED

KENDRAI MEEKS

ISBN-13: 978-1-953073-20-4

I

Tonight, the harvest moon would rise to tempt those who walked the night into its light.

IN ANOTHER THREE DAMNED HOURS. I still had nine minutes of my shift left, minutes which felt like sandbags. On the other side of the hour lay freedom, dancing, fires, and clan chanting. So much chanting. *Too* much. I looked at the Reagan-era clock that hung over my desk inside the ranger booth and grabbed the walkie from its charger on the window ledge.

"What do you want, Geri?"

"No one else is coming in. You and I both know this."

The speaker registered a few clicks before the main office hailed back. "The second we say okay to you closing early is the second Joe Detroit and his two-point-five kids roll in and want a campsite for the night."

I pressed the send button and my luck. "It's after Labor Day, Rick. The two-point-five kids are back in school and Joe Detroit is working a double at the stamping plant. Besides, it's freezing out. No one is going to want to get out of their cars and stare at a waterfall when it's this cold."

"It's Michigan, kid. You know how the camp crowd is. Neither rain nor sleet nor common fucking sense..."

The silent buffer filled the space between us.

Finally, I heard a click over the radio when my boss hit the send button. "Look, Red, if you want to leave early, just say 'I want to leave early, Rick.'"

"I want to leave early, Rick. You know you do too."

He groaned over the air, and I could practically picture his scruffy face crunching from the annoying reminder of how the moon pulled us both: me to my clan, and he to his pack.

"I guess you could..."

I didn't hear the rest. With speed that would have shocked a hummingbird, I had the shade down, the RANGER STAND CLOSED sign out, and my backpack slung over my shoulder. By the time I crossed the parking lot and entered the gift shop through the employee's entrance, Rick had shut down the main office too. Guess Joe Detroit was S.O.L. if he decided to show.

I quirked an eyebrow. By-the-regulations Rick wasn't the type to close-up shop early. A moment later, a scent on the breeze gave away the reason, but I played along. "Have I been that much of a bad influence on you?"

"Your mother was worried it was going to be the other way around, if I recall." He jerked his head towards the breakroom door. "I know you said you didn't want us to do anything, but you knew we weren't going to listen, right? It's not every day we send one of our kids off to the big city to go to school."

My hands flew up. "*Shhhh!*" Sneaking past him, I snuck a look around the edge of the door and tried to figure out based on sound and smell who was in the breakroom. My senses might pale in comparison to Rick's, but I knew this landscape well. If someone uncommon was on the premises, I'd pick it up.

Three bodies, all human. All other workers at the state

park. None of them my mother's informants.

Rick wore a know-it-all smile when I shrank back into view. "Still haven't told her yet, huh?"

"You know what my mom is like, and how pissed off she's going to be. I already get enough flack for me and Cody being friends."

"Friends? Is that what you kids are calling it these days?" Unconsciously, he crossed an arm over his chest and rubbed his opposite upper arm. "Don't take this the wrong way, kiddo, but I don't think I've ever met another woman more befitting of the name Brünhild."

"Amen to that."

When I was hired the summer after my senior year in high school, I thought the whole reason I got the job at the State Park was because everyone in town was scared shitless of my mom. *I'm* scared shitless of my mom. Rick, who was no doubt, scared shitless of my mom but hides it extremely well, proved that suspicion false on the third day of my employment, when she barreled into the gift shop, headed straight for his office, and told him in no uncertain terms that I would not be working there.

Rick just planted his fists on his hips, looked to the cash register where I stood trembling, and said to me, "Geri, if you were a minor, your mom would have every right to tell me you can't work here. At eighteen, though, the law considers you an adult. It's your call. You can quit like your mom here would like, or you stay on and learn how to do something other than terrorizing the local wildlife."

Eyes narrowed, finger pointed, and teeth grinding, Brünhild Kline had contemplated the man's murder, but knew where her domain ended and local labor laws began. "You've always had your nose wrapped up in other people's business, Rick Ryland."

Rick's nose had wrinkled as he bared his teeth at my mother. "Well, ain't that the pot calling the kettle black, *Matron*."

Running my hands under ice-cold water in the utility sink served two purposes: it washed away the grime that had built up from handling cash park patrons used for daily fees, and it distracted my brain from the buzz of hyper-awareness brought on by the approach of night. Normally, I'd never have worked on the day of a full moonrise, but desperate times called for desperate measures. The University of West Chicago didn't exactly accept pieces of silver for tuition. The inheritance sitting in the bank that I'd received from my paternal grandmother would pay for my classes, but I still had rent and living expenses to manage. Unless I wanted to live in Bessie, which frankly, wasn't out of the question. I'd practicing laying down in the bed of my truck many times, albeit not to *sleep,* and it wasn't half bad.

Be a hell of a lot colder without a werewolf to curl up next to, though.

Rick put his arm around me and pulled me along toward the breakroom. "Gale made her German Chocolate cake. Try to ignore how lopsided it is, okay? She worked really hard on it."

"I would never insult her cooking, Rick. You know that. Everyone here is like family."

"I know, kiddo. And we're going to miss you so much. Offer stands: you ever want to come back and work at the park over the summers, all you got to do is call."

"You sure this job is going to stay open?"

"As long as that river keeps flowing and the falls keep falling, the park will always be here."

II

Each curve pulled heavy on the steering wheel, though I knew it was just my imagination. My rust-kissed but solid bull of a Chevy pick-up had never let me down. Considering what the average Michigan wintertime in the Upper Peninsula entailed, that wasn't a trivial thing. No, the reason I felt like I was slowly wading into a vat of molasses was because of the angle of the sun puckering up to kiss the horizon in my rearview.

I should have been home by now. That my mother wasn't blowing up my phone meant that either her battery was dead or she was. I shouldn't have stopped at my storage unit on the edge of town, but there was no way I was taking a chance with hauling home the final supplies I'd picked up for Chicago.

Paradise was more of a zip code than a town; a halfway point between Tahquamenon State Park with its legendary waterfalls and Whitefish Pointe on the tip of the U.P., most famous for its Shipwreck Museum and its exhibit on the Edmund Fitzgerald. During the summer, many a tourist crossed through this Yooper oasis, but stopped just long enough to hit up the one bar in town and cut their name into its much-tagged countertop. As far as small towns went, it lived up to all the clichés. Legacies grew as thick as the oaks and willows that carpeted the gently rolling hills that rose out of Lake Superior. It was a canopy of expectation that had blocked out my view of the sun my entire life.

At the last intersection on the way home, I paused,

studying my options. I could turn left or right; both paths would take me out of town, away from home, and prevent the showdown with my mother. In both directions, the tall trees just beginning to blush with fall color and hit by the goldenrod rays of a fast-setting sun framed the roadway, like a mythic avenue of dreams. Ahead, the forest wove itself so tightly together that all I could see was shadow.

Running would imply that I was ashamed of what I was about to do. Though I feared my mother's reaction, I was not descended from fearful women. I would face her and stand my ground, taking whatever wrath she bore.

Besides, it was the last full moon at home, and the harvest moon at that. My skin crawled with anticipation for the fires. At the full moon's rise, my soul longed for the flame. How many lunar cycles in Chicago before the instincts deadened and I didn't feel this pull to clan and tradition?

My foot on the gas, I went boldly forward.

And that was when a flash of fur hit the hood of my car before rolling away to the side of the road.

III

I'd hit an animal; that much was apparent. But what kind? Out here, the possibilities could fill a zoo. Elk, moose, deer, bear? All possible, but given the hue of fur and the size of what had flashed before me, my suspicions were all but conclusive. Then, as I relaxed and connected with my senses, there was no doubt.

I pulled to the side of the road, cut the engine, and went for the utility box in the bed of the truck. Two gleaming silver blades met my eyes when I raised the lid, and next to them, my precious. A bow and arrow may have seemed a passé weapon-of-choice with all the firearms on the market today, but they had their upside. Light, portable, easy to shoot without riling up half the forest with the echo of the discharge. Plus, I just looked badass with one.

A bloodless trail relieved my immediate guilt that I'd severely injured something, but the consistently straight path concerned me. An animal just hit by a car should have been either limping from side to side, or instinctively weaving to avoid being pursued. As I got far enough into the forest that the light of day struggled to find ground, I realized either this animal didn't have the common-sense god gave a fruit fly, or I didn't. I looked back over my shoulder, but couldn't spot my truck through the growth. The thought of turning back crossed my mind only moments before the air from my lungs whooshed out as something slammed into me.

Face down on the forest floor, kissing dirt, an immense weight bore down and hot breath licked the back of my neck. The werewolf had me pinned.

Instinct ingrained by years of training and generations of breeding seized me. In moments, I took inventory of my situation. The ground provided a solid surface I could use to vault myself up. The bow was useless; my attacker would need to be in front of me. My best option would be to roll and hope the momentary shift of my body threw the wolf off balance. A few seconds would be all I'd need to access my weapons.

Overriding instinct however, I knew that my best option lay in ridicule.

My body went limp. "Most boyfriends just call when they want to talk, not throw themselves in front of their girlfriend's truck and give them a heart attack."

The balance of weight on my back shifted; brutish paws on my shoulder blades grew long and familiar. The wolf's hindquarters stretched, taking on their primate form. Soon, his long, muscular legs covered my own. His hipbones jutted into my lower back, followed by something definitively human, male, and solid.

"That's what huey boyfriends are like." Cody's voice, rough and airy and right against my ear, sent chills through my body. "But I'm not human, am I?"

He leaned forward, suckling my neck just below my ear. His touch stirred urges within, inspiring recollections what that mouth could do to other places on my body. We'd been rehearsing this dance for the better part of two years, a tenuous tango of desire and restraint. The full moon already hung low in the daytime sky and the primal instincts it triggered played havoc with willpower. Even as he shifted, Cody's hips rolled, making me suck in a breath and bite my bottom lip to quell my desires. One of us had to draw a line.

As usual, that would be me.

"You're moon mad, and I'm going to be late," I said. "If I don't get home, my mother will be combing these woods with a silver dagger etched with your name."

Unbothered, his teeth took to nibbling the bottom of my ear. "You want me. I can smell it."

Damn werewolves and their super senses. With a grunt and all my determination, I rolled. Cody could keep me down if he wanted; until I came into my full powers, any werewolf over the age of twelve could best me in a fair fight.

"Fine, let's do it," I said, teasing. "But you better make it one for the ages, because my mom will castrate you."

I barely paid any heed to the fact that he was naked as I stood up and leaned against a tree. I'd been around naked werewolves all my life – their human skin no less a layer of clothing over their true natures than a t-shirt or pants. Still, even I would admit that dynamic changed a little when the handsome, built, aroused male before you was your boy-friend.

"Really, castration? I've always pictured the Red Ma-tron as more of the disemboweling type."

Cody sat back on his heels, rubbing his forelegs and calming his hefty breathing. I tried not to notice how ripped he was, or think about how fun it would be to explore all those ridges and dips with my hands. It was too risky right now. Under the pull of a rising full moon, us being around each other was way too dangerous.

"I wouldn't put it past her." *Eyes above the belly but-ton, Geri!* "What are you doing out here, anyway? Doesn't your little werewolf handbook say you should stay close to the pack just before a full moon rise?"

He shrugged as he rose to his feet. "My uncle called me after you left work. Rick says you're planning on telling your mom tonight. I wanted to say good luck."

I ground my teeth. Wouldn't Rick have guessed that if I wanted my boyfriend to worry, I would have told him myself?

"I figured the rush of *feuernacht* would have her so giddy, she'd be a little less likely to skewer me."

Cody raised an eyebrow. "I don't think Brünhild Kline does giddy."

You should see her when she draws wolf blood, I thought. Instead of voicing my concern, however, I decided to distract my boyfriend by being all girlfriendish. Crossing to where he stood, suddenly looking sheepish, I rolled up on my toes and made doe eyes. "Thank you, Cody. That was really sweet."

He let my kiss land gently on his lips before his arms snaked around me and pulled me near. Like a racecar driver, I could count on his inner wolf to seize control of his libido this close to moonrise. Within moments, he'd deepened the kiss, his hands on my ass before drifting down and hitching under my legs, pulling me up.

"Too close... to full moon. Can't... Don't *want* to... resist you."

With every pause in his words, his hips undulated, tempting me with the promise of release even through the layers of my clothing between us.

"You have to. If you don't..."

Cody froze, pulling back to look me in the face, his gaze dripping with sincerity. "What if I don't?"

"Then you'll be bonded to me forever. You'll never be able to love another."

A quick peck of my lips, and he eyed me again. "I'm not

sure I'm capable of that now."

With my hands on his shoulders, I pushed myself away, reclaiming my own feet. "Cute, Cody, but the full moon can make a wolf say…"

Anger pulled his brow taut. All the passion that a moment before had been focused on seduction erupted. "It's not the full moon, Geri. Damn it, can't you see that…"

I flinched, shocked by the spike of anger, my hand instinctively wrapping around the hilt of the two-inch silver dagger braided into my hair. Cody's eyes focused on my defensive reaction with regret in his eyes. In a moment, he softened; both his tone, and his rigid muscles straining beneath his skin. He ran a hand through his messy brown locks in a wasted effort to tame them.

"It's not just because of the full moon. I've been thinking about this for a while. I'm… You know I love you, Geri, and you love me too."

I didn't deny it. I'd told him the first time a year ago and I'd never taken it back since.

Reaching for my hand, Cody pulled it to his mouth and planted a kiss. "Mate me."

My hand snapped back out of his, and I had to suppress myself from slapping him. "What in the hell are you talking about?"

"I'm talking about you and me, man and wife. I want you, Geri. I want you forever."

This amount of crazy should require a license. "Cody, I… I do love you. But I can't do that to you. I can't be the reason you lose your free will."

"That's the way we wolves work. It's just how we are," he argued, stalking me. I stepped back with each footfall of his forward. "At least with you, I'd know you're with me because you love me, not because some genetic mating imperative was forcing you to."

"You think it's that simple?" My back flattened against a tree. "*You're* a werewolf, *I'm* a hood. My kind balances your kind, with violence and death if it comes to that. Besides, I'm leaving for Chicago in three days."

He had a simple enough answer for that, one that to Cody seemed so ingenious and self-obvious, it had him grinning like an idiot. "Don't go then. Stay. Mate me. *Marry* me, or whatever it is you hoods do to seal the deal."

Cotton in my mouth and electricity passing through my tongue, a vision cracked across the edge of my imagination: me, naked underneath the confines of my red hood, straddling Cody while the wedding drums played and fires burned outside our tent. I could practically smell the ash and taste his kiss on my tongue as we consecrated our union, simultaneously both by my traditions and his.

He wore a knowing grin when my eyes opened, adjusting to the fast dying light of the forest at twilight. "Tell me yes, Geri. I'll make you the happiest shewolf in history. Plus, you know it would totally piss off your mom."

A bonus if ever there was one. And I couldn't deny that in the gentle moments of daydreaming when good sense and reality drifted away, I had pictured what it would be like to be Cody's wife. Those fantasies dissolved in the rays of day, when I looked in the mirror and could imagine myself cloaked in red and wielding silver, readying myself for the hunt.

"But I've planned for going to Chicago for so long." My last-ditch attempt at a justification to say no came out as more of a whine than a retort. "I worked so hard, Cody. Pulled straight A's at Community, saved up enough from work to make the trip, applied for entrance and got it, all without my mom finding out. To have done all that for nothing?"

"Fine, then we'll go to Chicago together." He tilted his forehead against mine. "As long as I come home for a few days around full moon, I'll be fine." His hands braced either side of my face. "Marry me."

All my kick-ass skills and abilities washed away in flood of girly glee. "I owe my mom the truth about Chicago first. Let me just get that out of the way, and then I can make a decision. Just give me a couple days, after the full moon and after the fires. Okay? I'm not leaving until the weekend."

"I waited this long for you, I can handle a few days more." He placed another kiss on my lips, this one the perfect balance of sweet and spicy. "She brought it on herself, you know. Your mother, I mean. Naming you after Little Red herself? She was practically tempting fate that you'd end up with a wolf."

That she was. That she was.

IV

Smoke rose from the trees, creating a plume that I could see a quarter-mile from the entrance to our property. Fall bonfires were commonplace here, the easiest and most efficient way to get rid of the carpets of leaves. Even though it was still early for such practices in mid-September, I doubted anyone would even notice. Hoods were backwoods folk, a necessity when charged with the policing, and when necessary, destruction of werewolves. We lived where they lived – away from civilization as much as civilization would allow.

In Chicago, I'd be alone. No hoods. No wolves.

Maybe an occasional vampire.

No slayers. They were all dead.

The twelve-foot gate that surrounded our compound would raise eyebrows in the lower peninsula, but in the U.P., privacy was respected. Did the locals know that behind those gates, in addition to a house, a barn, and garage, was a state-of-the-art training facility for the House of Red? Unlikely. Cousins, aunts, and uncles had their own homes and mini-compounds dotted across our territory, stretching from the Great Lakes to the Dakotas above the forty-fifth parallel, but the head of the operation and the command of the region lay with the Matron of our bloodline, my mother.

The gates clanged shut behind me, and I felt the weight of the cameras pivoting as Old Bessie started her way up the half-mile drive to the house. The smoke here was thicker, and the taste of it tickled my tongue and scratched at the back of my throat. Tonight's bonfire must have been bigger than usual. I needn't wonder why. As I got close enough to the house, a sea of trucks, SUVs, and smaller all-terrain vehicles formed a veritable parking lot. It wasn't unusual for a few family members to drive out for *feuernacht* and spend a few days reporting to my mother, but tonight it looked as though everyone had shown up.

Great, my mother would be distracted and wouldn't have the vaguest clue that...

"And just *where* have you been, Gerwalta?"

My mother's voice could crack lake ice in January. I dropped my car keys in the basket by the door and found myself trapped in the entryway. Leaning against a wall, Brünhild Kline met descriptions of both terrifying and beautiful. Her long black hair streaked with gray sat atop her head in a severe bun. Her ivory skin still held a touch of youth, though the lines on her forehead and at the corners of her eyes grew deeper by the year. Solid biceps flexed as she crossed her arms and glared at me, waiting for an answer, a scowl contorting a face that rarely knew smiles save when born of exacting pain on wolves or in the precious moments when my father could woo the little softness left within her.

"Like I said this morning, I had to work today."

"Yes, and you told me you were getting off at 5:30. It's nearly night now. Where have you been in the intervening two hours?"

The best way to lie to my mother was not to, to tell her only a partial truth and hope she didn't consider it worth her time to ask for more. "I ran in to Cody."

I bit my tongue before saying, *literally.*

"I know that much. I can smell the beast's stench all

over you." She straightened her back and arched an eyebrow. "And exactly what were you *doing* with the alpha's son?"

The same thing we always do, mother. Making out and dry humping and wishing we could sleep together without so many consequences.

And also, he proposed.

"Just talking."

"Just talking!" My words rebounded, coated in a layer of acid. "Can I remind you, daughter, that someday when *you* are the Matron of our bloodline, *he* will be your adversary. That you *talk* with him is concern enough. That you two are friends is something that must end."

I stared at the carpet, feeling as tall in my mother's eyes as the faded shag beneath my feet. "Maybe I don't want to *be* matron."

Without pretense, she delivered a response so well worn, the edges had lost all color.

"If not you, then who? All this — *all* of it, I have built for you. You are my sole heir, my legacy. You are the path by which the House of Red shall retain its rightful place in our world. You must be a worthy leader. A pack will never respect you if they know you once pined away for their alpha, and a pack that does not recognize our authority grows dangerous."

"An authority that does not respect its own limits and fails those it protects breeds revolution," I spat back through anger held down with leather straps.

"Spoken like a *modern* woman." My mother stepped closer, gaining strength in proximity and brewing fear with reserve. "Yours is not the world of modernity, Gerwalta. Yours is an old world of myth and chaos and death for those who forget their natures. What kind of hood would think something like that?"

"I'm not a hood," I reminded her. "Not yet."

She met my retort with a slow bob of her head. "No, you haven't taken your rites yet. I may have granted your father's request to wait until you finished with your college thing, but that's done now, isn't it?"

I'd finished my associate's degree at the local community college in June. That this hadn't come up before astounded me, but I chalked it up to a suspicion that my father wasn't quick to inform my mother. He'd been my passive ally since high school. Maybe it was only the change in the seasons and the lack of a new tuition bill that tipped her off. Maybe she didn't know at all and was only bluffing.

I resorted to partial truths. "Yes, I finished all my classes at community."

A cat-that-got-the-cream grin pulled taut the corners of my mother's mouth; she wore a smile born of my pain. "Then you're lucky that most of the clan just happens to be here for your cousin Robert's fire. He's proven to be not as difficult as you."

The fact that Robert was three years my junior, and my mother's passive aggressive insult meant to point out that truth, didn't allude me. The moment I visualized the building of the fire behind our house, of the clan chanting the sacred words and my cousin's form stepping into the heart of the blaze, of his body consumed by flame, burning away the traces of his humanity and leaving only that part of him which was beyond human, stirred primordial longing in me. I couldn't deny that I'd felt the pull of the consumption, even dreamed of my own fire. Inside, my nature called on me to take rites and claim my hood. But deeper, I wanted change, freedom, to know that I chose something out of will and not breeding.

Cody's words reverberated in my memory, reminding me why I'd really resisted my birthright.

At least with you, I'd know you'd fallen in love with me before we'd been together, not because some genetic mating imperative was forcing you to.

Going through rites would only enhance my genetic hardwiring. I wasn't sure I could think of him the same way on the other side of the fire. If I were to have any hope of marrying him...

"Then we should wait for next month," I said, desperate to find any way to get myself out of this corner. "A fire burns for only one hood. Tonight, that should be Robert. I can't usurp his moon."

"Agreed." My mother crossed her arms. "But I want you to remember how much this means to you, even as you attempt to deny it. Go to your room, you will not join us tonight."

Like the wolves communally taking their animal forms on the full moon, the hood was called to clan and fire. Just like a juvenile wolf, I had the ability to forgo the gathering if needed. But it would hurt. My insides would twist, my heart would race, and I'd feel a thirst for appeasement. It was the worst punishment my mother could bestow for daring to argue with her, but even more so because it would be the last time I was with my clan for months or even years to come.

In the blink of an eye, I reverted to my five-year-old self. "But that's not fair!"

"Is that your best defense?" she asked, cool as the moon in the autumnal sky, and just as distant. "Since when has fair had anything to do with my decisions? I am *just,* whether or not you believe I am fair. When you feel like your body is pulling itself in two tonight, remember that you brought this on yourself. Now go."

I remembered suddenly what I'd come home hoping to do before I'd been distracted. Before I could chicken out, I put my hand on her wrist and held her back.

"Wait! I want to talk to you about something. Not about *feuernacht* or my rites. It can wait, but maybe tomorrow?"

A slow drip of consideration in her eyes proceeded her response. "Very well."

With a nod, she was gone, leaving me to climb step by lonely step to my bedroom. Hopefully I could open my window and at least smell the fire. With any luck, I'd take part of its heat within me and be able to stand up my end of the conversation better with my mother in the morning.

V

Through the night, the revelry rang out. As the sounds of howls and hoots, laughs and claps, swish and swirl floated up to me through my cracked bedroom window, the draw of my clan tormented me. Damn my mother, and damn those born with the blessing of *not* being her daughter.

The upside of my punishment, however, was that come next morning, I was fully rested while *they* were not. Right after the rise of the sun, I crept downstairs, determined to sneak out before anyone was the wiser. I knew I'd be telling my mother about Chicago later on in the day but I needed to get out to nature to clear my head first.

I was just about out of the kitchen door, my truck keys in hand, when a voice dripping with Latin flavor spoke up.

"And where are you going so early in the morning?"

As central as my mother was wherever she happened to be due to her brawn and bluster, my father was her equal in cunning and stealth. I'd heard stories of how he snuck up on a lone wolf driven mad with lunacy and slit his throat. I wasn't exactly suffering lunacy, but I was definitely about to have my head handed to me on a silver platter.

"She didn't say I was grounded. She only sent me to my room."

My father pulled a languid draw of coffee, not saying anything, a tactic he knew worked with me. If left in silence, I'd out myself through babbling for every transgression.

"Nothing happened," I insisted. No need to say anything more than that. My mother would have informed him.

"You mean, nothing has happened *yet*."

"Just because Cody and I are friends…"

His hand jutted up, blocking my retort. What my mother did with glares, my father did with gestures. "Please, *boñita*, do not insult my intelligence. I've understood for some time that you and Cody and more than friends. I have tolerated it because I know you are wise, and I do not need to tell you how dangerous that game is."

I closed my eyes. I couldn't see the look on my father's face when I told him the truth. "I love him, Papa. I've loved him for a really long time."

When I dared look again, it was only to discover my bomb had failed to detonate. Instead, my farther fixed indifferent eyes on me. "So what? Does that change anything?"

"Of course it does. I mean, if the Matron of the House of Red and an alpha were in love with each other, don't you think that would ultimately be a good thing for wolf-hood relations? Think of how many conflicts we could resolve through dialog instead of violence."

"And think how many more conflicts such a union alone could inspire. An alpha is, first and foremost, answerable to his pack. Even before his own mate, the needs of the pack have priority. The first time one of them disagreed with his dictate, they'd blame it on you. He'd need to appease them, or they would challenge his leadership. Either way, he might die, and you would then likely do the same."

I didn't know what drove such boldness. "He's asked me to marry him."

For once, my cool and collected father bristled. "*Dios mio, porque no!*"

"Why is it so crazy? I'm not lying, Papa. We've never slept together. If Cody loves me, it's because *he* loves me."

"I forgive you for your daydreams. Ignorance and youth blind us, but a wolf and a hood can *never* be together. Remember what became of *Die Verräterin*."

Die Verräterin, the Betrayer.

My father couldn't have chosen a more impactful way to drive his argument home. I winced as the images filled my mind, a child's imagination sketching out the rougher details. Gerwalta Faust, after whom my mother named me, paid dearly for the greatest transgression a hood can commit: she married a wolf and bore him a child. While the fairytale painted her as a heroine trapped by naiveite, the real Gerwalta wasn't as fortunate as the Grimm Brother's Little Red Riding Hood. She, her wolf mate, and their child were skewered on silver spits and roasted alive while her matron – her own mother - chanted ancient incantations, relinquishing her powers so she could not defend herself.

"You don't need to tell me to remember," I said in softer tones. "I'm reminded each time I sign my name."

Stroking his beard, my father's head dipped. "She named you after The Betrayer so you could make the name one of pride again, not follow in her footsteps."

I had had enough of bearing the expectations of the three hundred years of hood that stood between me and my namesake. "Sorry, Dad. I guess that was a bad decision."

VI

Walden went to the woods to live deliberately; I went to the State Park where I had worked until only yesterday to live thoughtlessly.

In the measure of whom I loved more – my father or Cody – they were practically tied. Had it not been for my father's encouragement and willingness to have my back when my mother wanted to lash it, I'd probably have left home a long time ago. Not to run off to college and turn my back on all I'd known, necessarily, but at least to live with one of my cousins in Wisconsin, Ontario, or Montana.

As I followed the path toward the Upper Falls, I looked out on the rushing river, feeling the echo of my own struggle. For so many years, I had flowed along without conflict, letting the path I'd been born on move me. Then, as I became aware of my mother's sadism, and my father's tangential disavowal of her ruthlessness (to me in private, as he'd never openly question our clan's matron to anyone else), I began to rebel. I sped, I changed course, I rushed to jump over the edge.

I fell in love with a werewolf.

I stared at the falls before me, a series of aquatic plateaus cascading in seven different directions, and wondered which way to fall, and how much churning there'd be when I did. It took a few moments before I realized someone was talking to me.

I turned to see a woman, her head covered in dark cloth, biting her bottom lip.

I shook myself back to the moment. "I'm sorry, what?"

Her outstretched hand twitched again, offering her phone to me. "I said, would you mind taking a picture of us?"

Blinking away my inner thoughts, I smiled and took the device. When she backed to the railing and laced her fingers through the hand of a man wearing a yarmulke, I tried not to show the awkwardness I felt. I held up the Muslim woman's phone to square them in the frame with the mists of the waterfall rising behind them. Afterwards, the man moved on a few steps to get a better view as I handed the phone back to the woman.

Curiosity seized my tongue before I can stop it. "I'm sorry if I was gawking."

"Were you?" Her smile flickered. "No worries. We're used to getting looks. People don't expect to see a Muslima and a conservative Jew married to each other. We've learned to live beyond expectations, though."

An image of my father's anger-flecked eyes popped up in my mind. *A wolf and a hood can never be together.*

Because culture and history demanded it? Assumed it? Expected it?

Forbade it?

"I think that's..." I shoved my hands in my pockets. "... beautiful."

VII

It was time. Time to come to terms with everything I felt for Cody, and time to set out to do all I had decided to do with my life. Time to tell my mother about my relationship, about college, and that I'd decided to become the future alpha's bride.

I didn't need to take my fire to fuel the flames. I could make my own fire.

I'd accept what I wanted, stop feeling like it was something I had to hide or apologize for, and be a freaking adult. My mother's reaction wasn't my responsibility. If she wanted to summon her silver, skewer me, and roast me over the fires meant for my hooding, what could I really do to stop her?

All I had to do was find her and have done with it. In the training complex, I found one of the few cousins I considered a friend practicing his battle skills.

"Markus!"

The youngest of six siblings, Markus was the baby of his family, but "baby" was the last word anyone would ever use to describe him. Standing six foot three, he towered over me. When he wrapped me in his arms and spun me off the ground in his overly dramatic way, at least eight inches between my feet and the floor remained. He was a strong hood, one who took on his mantle at fourteen, the youngest of my generation. Once, my mother hoped I'd see him as a candidate for husband. Little did she know that Markus had been hoping to make a husband of our cousin Robert.

"There you are, Gerwalta. Why weren't you at the fire last night?"

He set me down like a feather on water, leaving me to straighten out my clothes. "Please don't call me that—it's Geri. And you know why. I was being punished."

"Your mother is mad at you again? Must be a day of the week that ends in y, then."

His light-hearted jab brought a much-needed smile to my face. "Speaking of the wicked witch, do you know where she is?"

"She was through here a little while ago, helping Robert adjust to all his new awesomeness and stuff. You should see his biceps ripple. I could watch that hood for hours." For a moment, Markus's face clouded over in a dreamy mask, and I tried not to picture what he must be thinking. Finally, he snapped back to attention. "Nope, she's not here. I thought I heard her say she had to go out for a summons."

My nose wrinkled. "A summons? I didn't know the wolves were having some sort of dispute that needed settled."

Markus grinned. "Just because you're tossing off the alpha's son doesn't mean you're the werewolf whisperer or anything. They're a large pack, Geri. Crowds create conflict. I'm sure it's nothing to worry about."

"I hope you're right. And just because I told you my secret doesn't me you can say anything about Cody and me around here. All the older hoods with their turbo hearing and stuff... Could get ugly if anyone finds out."

My cousin's eyes rolled. "You honestly think there's a single hood, wolf, or human in a ten-mile radius who doesn't know you two sneak off to the woods to polish bark all the time?"

I didn't want to ask what that term meant. "My mom doesn't."

"Right. You keep telling yourself that, and maybe sooner or later, it will be true."

VIII

I hovered in the kitchen until moonrise, only to be told by my father to go to my room and wait for my mother's return there. Early the next morning, after a sleepless twenty-four hours spent compiling mental lists, replaying the conversation by the falls, and listening to the sounds of my aunts, uncles, and cousins playing wargames inside the compound, I found myself and Old Bessie outside Cody's house. I didn't remember the drive, or even deciding to go. Something just... drew me there.

Cody's parents both worked in town during the day. I knew he would be home alone, if not only for the reason than we had taken advantage of that fact on several occasions. The spare key met my eyes when I opened the utility box panel on the side of the alpha's three-bedroom ranch house, its metal chilled from overnight temperatures that danced circles around the freezing point. I made my way for the back door, frosted leaves crunching beneath my feet.

"Screen door" was a symbolic name; I couldn't remember the last time it actually had a screen in it. Just beyond, I maneuvered the key to the keyhole and began to push it in the slot when I heard the sound of weather-stripping scraping wood. My eyes adjusted quickly to the dim light inside when I found the door unlocked and open.

"Cody?"

My voice deadened in a house strewn about with homemade afghans and carved wood knickknacks from local artisans. Carpet the colors of rocky road ice cream dampened the sound of my footfalls as I glided around furnishings and a stack of magazines piled up in the hall. Even though I was a nascent, a hood still not in command of all her strengths, I still had the innate abilities with which all my kind were born: stealth, agility, speed, superhuman senses. A *little* superhuman, anyway. Any righteous hood who'd gone through their rites would shoot past me on that one.

I moved through the interior of the house like mist over water. My hand on the open door, I paused, coaching myself for what I would do the moment I opened it and Cody set eyes on me.

I thought it over and you're right. We can make this work. Let's get married.

But I'm still going to college in two days, so we can get married in Chicago. For the moment, what do you say we just fuck and bond as a mated pair?

Okay, I might not use the term *fuck,* but damn it, there was no way either one of us was leaving this house a virgin.

I opened the door...

...and discovered one of us already wasn't.

The man who a moment before I had been ready to spend my life with, lay sleeping.

In the arms of another woman.

A naked woman.

I gave myself until the count of three, and proceeded to lose my shit.

"WHAT THE FUCK, CODY!"

Werewolves were gifted with speed that could make Olympic sprinters look like a child running through molasses in winter. One never could have guessed it from the way Cody's eyes languidly flickered open. Slower still was his ability to understand what was going on, or that he was currently using a brunette with half-inch blond roots as a blanket.

"Geri?" His hand slicked over his oily face. "What are you doing here?"

Just then, the shewolf began to show signs of life. Good, she was awake. That made it so much easier to kill her without guilt. *Run, bitch, run. Give me an excuse to chase you.*

"What am *I* doing here?" I vaguely motioned to the refuse on his bed. "What is *she* doing here?"

"Cody, sweetie, who is that?"

She had a voice, and judging by the amount of gravel in it, she'd been a smoker since she was in utero.

"Who am I? Who am *I?*"

Despite years of training to keep my emotions in check, my innate abilities were roaring to life through a vision of red. The shewolf's unkempt roots became my handle as I hoofed upon the mattress and dug my hand into her scalp, pulling her up to face me.

"I'm his girlfriend. Who in the hell are you? You're not one of the Paradise Pack, that's for hell sure. I know all of them."

Cody finally managed to sit up, pulling a fistful of twisted sheets and blankets over his lupine assets. He went from groggy to panicked in two seconds flat. "What the...? No, Geri, stop. Stop before you do something you're going to regret. Lisa is my..."

"Your what?" I demanded, waiting for the standard litany of male excuses to come pouring from his mouth. "Your sister? Your cousin? Your just-a-friend-and-it's-not-what-it-looks-like?"

"No, this is exactly what it looks like." My boyfriend's voice grew stern. The wolf shown through his eyes, sending a chill down my spine and loosening my grip. "Lisa is my..."

"I'm his mate!" The shewolf twisted away, crouching down in a position that would let her pounce and rip out my throat if she shifted forms. "I'm his wife, you crazy bitch."

My world.

Stopped.

"She's your..."

Tears, hot and as burning as the silent screams at the back of my throat, manifested at the corner of my eyes. A bare-backed Lisa began to rummage around the floor, picking up bits of clothing. Suddenly, the scene of what must have happened played itself out. Their touching. Their kissing.

Their mating.

Cody – *my* Cody – was gone.

"You're mated."

Whatever pity he could package together, Cody set it out in his features. "Yesterday we were joined, and this morning, we consummated. I've... We... Lisa, baby, can you give Geri and I just a few minutes?"

"Of course, sweetie." She had six pounds of sugar in a five-pound bag's worth of saccharine goodness in her grin as she leaned over the mattress to press a kiss against Cody's mouth, her ass pointed my direction. "I'll just go jump in the shower."

Lisa didn't worry that I'd negotiate my heart. She didn't worry that I'd try to make Cody see why this was all wrong. She didn't have to worry that my tears and my suffering would tug his heartstrings and bring him back to me.

She didn't have to worry about anything. They were mated, sealed in an eternal mystical bond, one that would last until death.

One that was supposed to have been ours.

"You're mated." I repeated the words as though comfort could be found in the stark truth, but it wasn't. I'd decided to turn my back on my family, my traditions, my birthright if needed, all to be Cody's wife. For nothing. "How? Why? When?"

"My father…" Cody shrugged. "Alpha's prerogative."

"Oh."

I didn't need any more explanation than that. Cody was a werewolf, and his father, not only the man he held above all others as a role model, but his pack's alpha. If his father were to decree that Cody would take a particular mate, he wouldn't have a choice. When the alpha gave a firm command, the packling had only two choices: obey or leave the pack. One kept you alive, the other could trigger a chain of events that ended in insanity and execution by hood.

"But why would he… Your dad has been… He *liked* us."

He liked *me*.

It didn't make sense. Cody's father hated the concept of alpha's prerogative. He boasted about how rarely he exercised the option. Their pack was made of wolves descended from Swedes and Finns. Like their human countrymen, they'd come to the new world with beliefs in hard work and community rule. When Michael Ryland put his paw down, it was only because he had no other choice.

Scooting to the end of the bed, Cody secured the sheets around his waist. Never mind that I didn't need a live model to recreate every inch of his body in my mind's eye.

"I know this is tough for you, Geri. Hell, it's tough for me. I fought my dad on it when he tried to get me to accept it of my own free will. When he ordered me, I did what he wanted, but inside, I was screaming for you. But the moment Lisa and I…" He had the nerve to blush, tucking his chin into his shoulder. "Then I knew she's the one I'm supposed to be with. She's the only one I could ever be with. I love her. I love her more than…"

A sickly suspicion began to leak in to the cracks of my horror. My hand shot up, killing his momentum. "Did he say why?"

Confusion marred his tragically beautiful brow. "What?"

"When you told your dad that you didn't want to mate Lisa. Did you tell him it was because you'd just proposed to me earlier in the day?"

His hand scratched the scruff at the back of his neck. "I told him I loved you. I told him that I only wanted to be with you."

"But another shewolf from another pack just *happened* to roll into town." The same time my extended family had come in from all corners to witness Robert's fire, leaving behind their own packs. Thunder rumbled in my chest as I leapt off the cliffs of my conclusion. "Did you mention you were planning on running away to Chicago with me and you'd only be home for full moons?"

Slack-jawed, Cody shook his head. "I didn't get that far. He told me in terms that left no room for discussion that you and me were through. He forbade me to talk about you until Lisa and I were joined."

The last twig of my patience snapped. "I have to go."

The shower in the bathroom came on just as I turned

on my heel and started to march out of the room. I'd put down four steps when Cody's hand on my shoulder stopped me. I couldn't turn around, even though I knew inherently he wanted me to. No matter how this happened, and despite the fact that he was a werewolf, Cody Ryland was a good man. He wouldn't let me walk away thinking *I'd* done something wrong.

"You're a beautiful, intelligent, kickass woman, Gerwalta Kline, and any man—wolf, hood, or huey—would be lucky to have you. If there's ever anything I can do, anything at all..."

His voice trailed off, dragging the shreds of my hopes and dreams of our life together with it.

"Cody, I..." I couldn't get it out. No matter how much I longed for reciprocity, I wasn't there yet. I may never be there. To tell him that I wished he and his new mate well would be a lie. Deep down, I wanted to see them suffer. I wanted my heart to be avenged. I wanted to feed Lisa's blood to my silver blade and hear Cody's keening howl, knowing I took his mate from him.

I wanted to take my rites, let the fires consume the old me, and come out a righteous hood on the other side so I could have justice.

I wanted to become everything my mother wanted me to become.

I wanted to become my mother.

My chest fell as I exhaled my frustration, knowing there was only one place to turn, one person responsible for what had happened.

"No, Cody. There's nothing you can do. Good bye. Good bye forever."

IX

I flew into the house. A gaggle of cousins and two of my aunts in the living room barely registered as they called out, trying to get my attention. I had no interest in playing junior hostess. I needed to see my mother and I needed to see her now.

Brünhild looked like she'd been expecting me when I entered her formal office at the back of the house. Her hand wrapped around the handle of her favorite stein, one that depicted a pack slaughter in the Black Forest. One knee-high boot crossed over the other as she sat in her carved wooden chair, her gaze fixed on me at a distance. I stood at the door, my chest heaving, my thoughts racing, blood boiling.

"Out with it now, Gerwalta. We both know why you think you're here."

"Why I *think* I'm here?" Pain barely registered as my nails pressed so hard into the heels of my hands, I swore that blood must be running. "How could you, Mother? *How could you?*"

"How could I?" She repeated my question in a repulsed tone dripping with scorn. "What did you expect me to do? Allow you to go off and become some wolf's bitch? I didn't name you Gerwalta so you could repeat the same mistakes."

She rose slowly, like a queen staring down one of her unruly subjects, before stalking toward me. "Someday, you will command of our bloodline, and if you prove worthy,

Grand Matron. A righteous hood of the House of Red *cannot* rule while opening her legs every night to the enemy."

I took two steps forward, meeting her glare with every ounce of fury I could muster. The *thwack* my flying hand made when it met her stoic face echoed off crimson papered walls, off the wood and stone hearth where a fire danced with an intensity that matched my own. My mother was my superior in every way; she could have stopped my assault midair had she wanted. Though I was curious why she didn't, I pressed forward, not knowing how much longer my luck would hold.

"This goes far beyond what you've done to me. What gives you the right to interfere in pack dynamics that way? What in the hell did you threaten Michael Ryland with to get him to command Cody to mate someone he didn't have any feelings for?"

"I didn't *command* any one. I only *advised* Michael that if his son ever attempted to bed a member of my bloodline, I'd have his pelt for my bedclothes. I suggested that Cody might consider taking a mate with a great deal of urgency. Luckily, my sister had already brought Lisa Kepler from the Ely Pack, who was hoping to find a match here in Paradise. How the alpha interpreted and acted on those suggestions was his own concern."

"That's what flies for diplomacy in your eyes? Threatening wolves you're charged with overseeing with death if they don't obey, and calling it their free choice when they kowtow?"

Her hands folded before her, she nodded. "If I cannot control an alpha wolf, I cannot control any wolf. And if we cannot control the wolves, they will grow wild and feral. Remember that we don't exist simply to make their lives difficult. Once upon a time, werewolves and vampires openly hunted defenseless humans, killing and consuming without limit. Slayers and hoods came into the world to make certain *every* species which shares it had protection from the others. When you're matron, you'll be wise to remember this."

"When I'm…" The words died in my throat. "I will *never* be matron, I'll never be a hood of your clan."

"We are what we are. Becoming a hood isn't a choice. It's an imperative. Becoming the matron isn't a birthright, it's the very reason you breathe and live. Enough!"

In a swish of arms, my mother beckoned her full power. The air sizzled with old magic, filling the room with the scent of pine needles and damp oak. Dressed in her common black hunting boots, black jeans, and ruby red button-down, her amber eyes flooded silver. Tendrils of power slicked back over her hair, down her shoulders, and blanketed her back, solidifying into a red cloak, the cloth that had given our kind our names.

"I grow tired of your insolence. It is time for you to pass through the fire and become one of the righteous."

Panic punched me in the gut. "That's why the family is all here, isn't it? It wasn't just for *feuernacht*. It wasn't just for Robert's hooding; they could have done that at any of the family compounds. It wasn't even as a cover to bring in a shewolf that you could force on Cody. You want them here as a sort of coronation."

"It's far more than that, child. I wanted them here in case there was need to hold an inquest," my mother said, standing tall. "If Cody could not bed the shewolf, I would have known that you'd blackened your name and lain with him. With the witness of the family, I would have ordered you to carry out the sentence and cut his throat."

The image of that fate made me see red. "I would never… *Never* hurt Cody."

"Oh, really?" My mother's eyebrow arched. "Don't tell

me that when you found him in the arms of another, you did not want to see his blood flow from his veins."

She caught the guilty flash in my eyes before I was able to turn away.

My mother preened her cloak. "As I said, we are what we are. A hood's nature is to *destroy* a wolf, not seduce one. Ask yourself, why hadn't you slept with him? It's because, in your soul, you are repulsed by the idea. Stop trying to reclaim the shame of your forefathers. Take your fire, and your rightful place at my side as the Grand Matron-in-training."

If I breathed deeply enough, I could taste how the magic scented the air, how it called to me to accept it in to my body. My mother was right about that much: *this* is what I was by birth. The power, the magic, the ability to run in time with werewolves, command silver to do my bidding, even fly if I was one of the lucky few gifted with the ability, was there for me to claim. All it would take would be my submission, and the elders of my clan calling on the ancient power that would grant me my own hood and imbue my body with the strength of my ancestors. In time, my ability, the respect and fear among both hood and wolves would equal that of my mother, maybe even surpass it.

I could think of no more horrid a fate.

"No."

"No?" Brünhild faltered. "What do you mean, no?"

I backed toward the door. "I would have refused to kill a man whose only supposed *crime* was loving me. I refuse to twist the hearts and minds of good wolves to further my political standing. I refuse to be like you. I *am* nothing like you."

"Oh, aren't you?" With her power, she beckoned a silver plate sitting on the fireplace. It sailed through the air, simultaneously morphing, reforming itself through my mother's unspoken command. When it hit her hand, what had been a simple round disc took on the form of a short sword. My mother held it up, the tip angled at my chest. "Which of us carries the greater shame from what you've done? You accuse me of being horrendous for simply getting your wolf to follow through on his instincts, while you spent two years drawing him away from his nature to get away from yours. Ask yourself, did you ever really love him, or did you just love the idea of doing something to piss me off?"

Even I couldn't deny that had been part of Cody's appeal in the beginning, but it had quickly grown into so much more than that.

"I was ready to be his wife."

"You were ready to be his doom. A hood and a wolf can never be together. *Never.* Our instincts to destroy each other are too great. Marrying Cody would only have set one or both of you up for an early death."

"At whose hands, mother? Mine, or yours?"

"They are the same hands." She raised her sword between us, the blade tip just inches from my heart. "Now, listen to me and listen well, daughter. I have tolerated your childishness and hesitance long enough. We are going downstairs now, and your aunts and I will summon the fire so that I can bestow your rites on you. You *will* pass through the flames. If you do not, I will gather our clan and destroy not only your precious Cody, but the entire Paradise clan."

The knob turned in my hand as my head lowered, eyes cast to the floor. "Yes, Matron. I will prepare for the ritual immediately."

I knew an empty threat when I heard one. Part of the reason that my mother held such a lofty position in our society was that her actions were firmly rooted in reason. Reasoned actions delivered with a silver-plated fist, perhaps, but she knew how hard she could press her position and when to pull back.

The ultimatum had not been given by Brünhild the Grand Matron. It was by Brünhild, the mother who felt she had no other options.

She might be right when it came to Cody; the community would probably back her slaying him if we actually had been together. But the whole pack? I knew there was no reason even she could conjure that would demand such retaliation, especially given that Cody was now mated to one of his own kind.

The werewolf threat had been neutralized. The threat from within – me, the rebellious hood – remained. I wasn't safe here anymore.

X

An old duffle bag became my impromptu suitcase. I wouldn't need much from here; I'd spent the last three months serendipitously gathering what I would need when I moved to Chicago and putting it in a storage locker Rick owned. Earlier in the week, I'd even drained my bank account — a bank account my mother didn't know existed — in preparation for leaving. The plan had been to skip town three days past full moon, after *feuernacht,* when the pull of my instincts would be on the downslide. And coincidently, two days before fall classes at the University of Southwest Chicago started.

Waiting wasn't an option anymore. I had to go, and go *now*, before the aunts came to escort me to the ceremony.

I had just zipped up the duffle when a knock turned me into ice. I stuffed the bag under my blankets, hiding the bulge with my body just as the door opened and my father walked in.

"Your mother said that you've finally agreed to the ritual. I came to see if—"

The pride in my father's eyes, shining as bright, died when he saw me. I saw then that he'd donned his own yellow hood, giving him away as a hood from the Casa de Amarillo. I'd always found it curious that for all my mother's arrogance about the House of Red, she'd married a man from a different clan. Shame wrinkled the edges of my resolve. In the closet, my formal *feuernacht* gown hung untouched. He took one more look at me, then at it, then me again.

He took the dress down, carried it over to me before gently attempting to hand the garment over. "Quickly. Your aunts are already building the fire."

I may have summoned the guts to lie to my mother, but I didn't hold enough animosity for my father to repeat the deception.

"I'm leaving."

"Leaving?" His brow wrinkled. "I don't understand. What's going on? What happened?"

"Did you know?" I couldn't bring myself to look at him, afraid what I might see. "About what she was going to do to Cody?"

My father's brow wrinkled. True concern shown in his features. "What happened to Cody?"

"Ask your wife, it's an engaging story." I peeled back the blankets, grabbed my bag, and flung it over my shoulder. "I'll be in Chicago; I'm not sure where. I'll call when I figure things out, but don't expect me to come here again."

"Chicago? *Cariño*, you can't be serious. You're a hood. How will you survive in such a big city, and with nothing but your innate abilities?"

"I guess the way everyone else does. Like a human."

POSTLUDE

Pietro Kline observed his wife's hooded silhouette against the massive, riving bonfire. He'd known a number of bloodline matrons in his life, first in his own clan in his native Argentina, then others as he migrated north when circumstances forced him from his homeland. When he'd caught a red hood's eye, one in line to lead her clan, it had been a shock, not only to himself, but to his mother and father as well. Yellow hoods had a reputation of being gentler with the wolves under their command, of preferring negotiation and diplomacy to solve problems and only resorting to the hunt when all other routes had been exhausted. The reds...

No other bloodline's cloak better matched their nature.

Their daughter had always embraced the extremes of their contradictory natures. He'd anticipated high expectations for any offspring wrought of their union... But how high sometimes took him aback. Pietro walked a fine line, between being his child's champion, being his wife's partner, and being the matron's second.

Brünhild glanced back momentarily over her shoulder, before returning her eyes and her concentration to the fire. "When will she be down?"

He side-eyed the nearby members of the clan gathered to observe the sacred rites, and stepped closer, leaning in over his wife's shoulder from behind. "Never."

Each of Brünhild's knuckles popped in sequence, but

her voice remained a smooth plateau of emotion. "She's running."

"What did you think would happen if you backed her into a corner? You know who—and *what*—she is." Pietro heard the chastisement creep into his voice and aimed to soften it. "Our daughter hasn't changed. She's as unwavering and as unmovable as you. You won't hear from her again, Brünhild. Not until she decides it's time."

Brünhild clicked her tongue. "She can run from us, but she cannot run from her nature. It's welling up inside her, Pietro. I feel it. *She* feels it. Her destiny is calling to her, and its voice is getting louder. She will come to the fire soon enough. And if she does not, the fire will come for *her*."

THE STORY CONTINUES IN
THE RED CHRONICLES
BOOK ONE – RELUCTANT.

Would you like to keep up on Kendrai's other projects and appearances, and get updates on releases and insights into her writing?

Check out how at:
www.kendraimeeks.com

MEEKSOLOGY:

RED CHRONICLES*:

REQUITED - PREQUEL

RELUCTANT - BOOK ONE

RELINQUISHED - BOOK TWO

RAVENING - BOOK THREE

REBELLIOUS- BOOK FOUR

RIGHTEOUS - BOOK FIVE

RED ORIGINS*

BEAUTY & THE BETRAYER - BOOK ONE

THE WOLF & THE WATCHER - BOOK TWO

RED & THE RESTORER - BOOK THREE

ENTER THE KINGDOM*

COURT OF DISCONTENT - PREQUEL

MISTRESS OF CINDERS - BOOK ONE

FREEBIRD - SIDE STORY

ISLE OF AFTER - BOOK TWO

VAMPIRE SOVEREIGNS

VENICE DUSK - BOOK ONE

* Complete Series.